To Carter,

I L♥ve You,
a Bushel and a Peck!

From

....

Carter, you're my everything!
I love you more each day.
From dawn till dusk, you make me proud
in every single way.

Carter, you're a joy to watch.
I love to hear your laughter.
You are the sunshine in my life—
my happy ever after!

Carter, you're the sweetest soul.
I've loved you from the start.
Wherever you go, I'll be near,
you're always in my heart.

Carter, I'm in awe of you.
I love to watch you grow.
You make me feel so happy—
more than you will ever know.

Carter, you're so wonderful.
I love each day we share.

Together, we can do so much.
We make a perfect pair.

Carter, I love your caring ways.
You're super-kind and sweet.
Sing, dance, be kind, have fun!
The world is at your feet.

Carter, you're my precious one.
I love to snuggle you.
I cherish all the times we share,
and everything we do.

Carter, I adore you,
and our love grows more each day.
You're my extra special gift,
I'll always feel this way.

Carter, you're my shining light.
I love your sense of fun.
I'm happy that you're in my life—
our journey's just begun.

Carter, I feel so lucky
when I'm spending time with you.
I'm delighted with all you say,
and everything you do.

Carter, you're my shooting star.
You mean the world to me.
I love you, a bushel and a peck!
You're all I dreamed you'd be.

Carter, you're my everything!
I love our time together.
Each day, each night, I love you more—
now, always, and forever.

Carter,
**We L♥ve You,
a Bushel and a Peck!**

Written by Louise Martin
Illustrated by Jo Parry
Designed by Ryan Dunn

Copyright © Bidu Bidu Books Ltd 2024

Published by Put Me In The Story,
a publication of Sourcebooks.
P.O. Box 4410, Naperville, Illinois 60567-4410
(630) 536-1104
putmeinthestory.com

Date of Production: August 2023
Run Number: 5033220
Printed and bound in China (GD)
10 9 8 7 6 5 4 3 2 1

FSC
www.fsc.org

MIX
Paper | Supporting
responsible forestry
FSC® C117745

put me
in the story®
Bestselling books starring your child!
putmeinthestory.com